I0780606

Fiend Hunters

By

Angel Rocio

Angel Rocio

Copyright © 2025

All Rights Reserved

No part of this publication may be reproduced, distributed, or transmitted in any form or by any means, including photocopying, recording, or other electronic or mechanical methods, without the prior written permission of the publisher, except in the case of brief quotations embodied in critical reviews and certain other noncommercial uses permitted by copyright law.

ISBN: 978-1-966642-59-6

Dedication

I like to dedicate this novel to my family, and to authors like Gege Akutami, Koyoharu Gotouge, and Chu Gong, too. My family has been so supportive of my dream of becoming an author, and I am so grateful to them. And I believe if I had never read books by authors like Gege Akutami, Koyoharu Gotouge, and Chu Gong, I won't have made my novel. Their novels inspired me to make this novel and to become an author. I am so grateful again for my family and authors, thank you.

Angel Rocio

Acknowledgment

I would like to thank the team at NYpublishers.co for everything. Without them, this novel would have never happened, and without them, my dream of becoming an author would have never happened. I am very grateful for NYpublishers.co.

Table of Contents

Dedication iii

Acknowledgment iv

About the Author vi

Arc 1: 1

To become a fiend hunter 1

Chapter 1: The Abandoned Asylum 2

Chapter 2: The Beast Within 9

Chapter 3: An Unexpected Guest 13

Chapter 4: The Fiend Hunter Headquarters 20

Chapter 5: What Are Fiends? 28

Chapter 6: Training to become a Fiend Hunter 33

Chapter 7: The Fiend Hunter Meeting 39

Epilogue 46

About the Author

vi

My name is Angel Rocio, I like to read novels, comics(Graphic novels, manga), and historical books too, but my favorite books are Jujistu Kaisan, Demon Slayer, Solo Leveling, and RE: zero- starting life in another world from zero are my favorite manga, I also like video games ranging from open world, and a singular storyline games.

Arc 1:

To become a fiend hunter

Chapter 1: The Abandoned Asylum

"The fall breeze is so gentle," said William.

"I know," said Jen.

Jen and William have known each other for at least a year. They met in their English class the past year, they became friends because both of them like the paranormal, they like to explore abandoned places after school, and they like to explore them with other friends too.

"Hey, Jen, want to explore an abandoned place after school with Ben and Clara?" said William.

"Sure," responded Jen.

Later, William can hear Ben tapping his fingers on his desk. William and Ben have been friends ever since the beginning of freshman year. William can tell Ben is in his own little world right now because of how bored he is.

"Hey Ben," said William.

No response from Ben.

"Hey Ben," said William again, but again no response.

"BEN!" shouted William.

Ben jolted, "What, what happened?" said Ben.

"What happened? You look dead, man I had to do something before you died from boredom," said William.

"Dude, you could've just let me die from boredom instead of being here in school, and learning about English," said Ben.

"Anyways, are you ready to head to the abandoned building after school?" said William.

"I'm ready, and I got all the equipment we need, too," responded Ben.

William asks, "What time will we be going to the abandoned building?"

"I believe 6:30 is the perfect time to head to the building," responded Ben.

"That's fine with me," says William.

Later the same day,

"Damn, it got a bit colder now," said Jen.

"What did you expect? It's fall, it's colder when the sun isn't out," responded William.

"Are Ben and Clara waiting for us at the abandoned building?" said Jen.

"I believe they're there now, I think?" responded William.

In the distance, William and Jen can see Clara and Ben waving and smiling at them, and William and Jen do the same back at them.

"Okay, who is ready to head inside the building?" Ben says.

"WE ARE!" responded the others excitedly.

They were careful when they entered the building so that they wouldn't get injured or get caught in it. Looking around with flashlights, they find a lot of graffiti on the walls. Going forward, they find there are two paths in front of them.

"I will go with Jen to the left side, Ben and Clara, you guys can head to the right side," says William.

Ben responds, "Ok, I'm fine with that, but let's hope that we find each other at the end of the paths we don't want to get lost."

They then proceed to the paths they planned to enter. Further along the path, Jen and William find more graffiti on the walls, but it looks even more terrifying. The graffiti features some disturbing writings on the wall, along with drawings that give the appearance of demonic beings, but Jen and William continue further.

On the other path, Ben and Clara find graffiti that resembles what William and Jen found on the walls as well.

"Hey Ben," Clara says.

"Yeah?" Ben responds.

"Do you know what this place is?" asks Clara.

"Yeah, this place used to be an asylum. Why do you ask?" says Ben.

"Just wanted to know," responds Clara.

But, just then, they smell a foul odor and see a room in the distance. They continue, and when Clara and Ben enter the room, they are shocked and terrified by what they see. Still, beside those bodies, they saw some type of shrine that had demonic symbols on it, but the most terrifying thing was that there were heads that were placed upon sticks right next to the shrine.

"We have to get out of here," said Ben in a whisper.

But then, in the distance, they saw a monster coming out of another room in front of them.

Just then, Ben shouted, "WE HAVE TO GET OUT OF HERE!"

In a panic, Ben and Clara ran out of the room as fast as they could.

On the other side of the building, William and Jen found a shrine with demonic figures on it, and on the shrine, there appeared to be writing. Still, on that writing, they saw that blood was used to write the words on the shrine, but just then a demonic-looking monster jumped out of a corner, and started to run towards William and Jen.

William and Jen start to run away from the monster, but the monster grabs Jen by the leg and hangs her. William, in desperation, charges up his punch and jabs the monster, but the monster stops the punch and breaks William's arm, then throws him away through the walls.

Just then, Ben and Clara arrive to see that there is a monster that is hanging Jen over its mouth. Ben and Clara panic, thinking that they're going to die here, but they sense a strong force in the direction of a dark hole. Coming out of the dark hole is William, with damaged clothes and a broken arm. Still, just then, his arm starts to heal like it was never broken.

Ben, in fear, says, "William looks pissed off now."

Chapter 2: The Beast Within

William runs toward the monster that has Jen dodging every attack that the monster throws at William, William kicks the monster arm ripping in the process, and putting Jen on the ground next to Ben and Clara, William ran at the monster so fast that it looked liked he teleported William punches the monster with so much force that it blasts away breaking through walls. William turns his head, looking at the monster that is about to hit him. William dodges the attack and starts to attack the monster with combos, jabs, hooks, kicks, and the final attack with an upper cut that rips the head of the demonic monster, killing it in the process. But then the monster from before sneaks up on William, tackling him through other rooms and throwing him. William hits the ground, but catches himself.

William charges at the monster with rage, the monster charges at William with murderous intent, and William and the monster start attacking each other, punching and blocking. Both the monster and William are equal in strength and speed. Ben can't even see William's movements. William hits the monster with a right hook that blasts the monster away, hitting the ground.

William appears right beside the monster and hammer punches the monster on its back, making an indent on the ground. Then, William grabs a large piece of debris and crushes the upper half of the monster, killing it. William turns around, looking at his friends walking towards them, but suddenly the floor starts to rumble, then from behind William is a Demonic monster that stands 15ft taller than William.

The demonic monster looks so hideous and terrifying, and the skin of the monster looks smooth and tough like an exoskeleton of a cockroach. He is also wielding a chain with a sharp, curved hook that resembles a fishing hook.

Then the monster spoke, "Are you the chosen?"

"What?" responded William.

The monster said again, "Are you the chosen?"

"I don't know what you're talking about," says William.

Then the monster says something that confuses him.

"You have to be the chosen because you have the same aura as my king," says the monster.

William asks, "Who is your king?"

The monster responds, "My king is Lucifer, the KING OF FIENDS!"

William and his friends are in disbelief at what they heard, then the demonic monster says, "My king told me that one day there will be someone who will be as strong as him, he told me that they will be called the chosen. But the kicker here is that the person who is picked as the chosen has to be a descendant of his family, which means YOU ARE THE DESCENDANT OF THE KING OF THE FIENDS!!!!"

William was completely shocked by what this demonic monster said. He wanted to ignore what the demonic monster said, but then it spoke again.

"You have the same ability as my king; you are currently using an ability similar to my king called demonic rage, but it seems like you can't control it like my king; however, it seems like you have another presence within you. Perhaps there is a beast within you."

Chapter 3: An Unexpected Guest

"Oh yeah, apologise, how can I be so rude, I haven't even introduced myself, My name is Beelzebub, now what is your name, human trash?" says the demonic monster.

"The name's William Asher, and I'm going to beat your ass."

William was getting ready to attack the demonic monster. William witnessed the monster disappear in the blink of an eye. Just then, William felt a strong presence behind him. William, turning his head, can see that the demonic monster has appeared right behind him. Before William could react, Beelzebub punched William, blasting him away onto a wall, making an imprint on the wall.

Beelzebub runs toward William, punching him rapidly, then William is thrown, hitting the ground, then Beelzebub appears beside William, then hammer fisting him to the ground. Beelzebub grabs William, choking him to death, but William uses his rage technique to kick out of Beelzebub's grasp. William then punches and tornado kicks, and back kicks, and finally hits Beelzebub with a strong right hook that blasts Beelzebub away, crashing through a wall. William turns to look at his friends walking towards them, just then, from behind, "That was fun. But you're weak, human," Says Beelzebub. Then Beelzebub ran so fast that he appeared in front of William, punching William on the stomach. William threw up blood, getting blasted to a wall, crashing on it, and falling unconscious.

Ben witnesses the battle, looks at Clara, then says, "We have to do something to at least slow down that monster."

"But, what can we do? We don't have any abilities like William," responded Clara, Ben, and Clara.

Then they looked around to see what they could do to slow down the monster, and then they saw a part of the building that looked like they could push on the monster. William regains consciousness, looking at Beelzebub walking towards him.

"You are so pathetic. I believed when I sensed your aura, I thought that I was going to fight the chosen, but I was wrong, you're just a pathetic human," said Beelzebub.

Beelzebub was ready to throw his weapon at William to kill him. Still, just then, he saw a part of the building leaning toward him, collapsing on top of Beelzebub, Ben, and Clara from a distance, happy and relieved that they had stopped that monster. "Get Jen and run, I'll go and help William," said Ben.

"Ok," responded Clara.

Ben ran to William, but felt like something was off, like it wasn't over. When he reached William, he made sure that William regained his consciousness. "William, wake up," said Ben. "William, wake up, we have to go now."

Ben could see that William was trying to open his eyes. In relief, he grabbed William's hand and pulled him up, and led him to the wall.

"William, you think you can walk?" asked Ben.

"Yeah… I think," responded William.

"Ok, that's good, but that was badass, man, that battle looked like something out of some movie," said Ben William.

Ben started laughing. "But, thankfully, you're fi-."

Ben and William looked at Ben's chest and saw a hook impaled through Ben's chest. Blood started to come out of Ben's mouth and chest, then Ben said, "William…help me."

Then Ben was pulled toward Beelzebub. While Chucking Beelzebub said, "You all thought that you could kill like that, oh, how stupid humans like you are, but at least I have a snack here."

Then Beelzebub opened his mouth, revealing his sharp teeth, and ate Ben. William could only watch as Beelzebub was consuming Ben. Blood was being spilled all over the ground. In a rage, William runs at Beelzebub, charging up his right punch at him, but Beelzebub stops the attack, then Beelzebub tears William's arm off in agony. William falls onto the ground. William looks up at Beelzebub in fear.

Beelzebub raises his weapon to kill William. Suddenly, a person appears and cuts Beelzebub's arm off in a lightning flash. Beelzebub charges up his punch to hit this person, but he dodges the attack and tornado kicks Beelzebub away, but catches himself. Beelzebub starts to chuckle.

"You're strong. What's your name, human?" asks Beelzebub.

The man then says, "My name is Yazen, Yazen Alexander, the strongest Fiend Hunter of this era."

Beelzebub starts to chuckle, and he then regenerates his arm. Yazen and Beelzebub then brace themselves. At that instant, both Yazen and Beelzebub ran toward each other, punching and dodging attacks.

Yazen is so fast that he's dodging all of Beelzebub's attacks. Beelzebub is amazed by how fast Yazen is. Yazen then hooks and kicks Beelzebub, blasting him away. Beelzebub catches himself suddenly. Yazen hits him with two jabs, two hooks, and a strong upper cut that has electricity blasting Beelzebub up to the air, then Yazen hammer kicks Beelzebub, hitting the ground, creating a crater on the ground. Yazen charges up a left punch; however, Beelzebub moves out of the way quickly.

Yazen hits the ground, missing Beelzebub. "You are magnificent, Yazen, you are the strongest of this era," says Beelzebub while chuckling.

"You're strong yourself, but it's time to kill you," says Yazen. Yazen then charges up a lightning ball in his hand to blast Beelzebub; however, before Yazen can blast him with his lightning, Beelzebub teleports out of the area.

Yazen, in frustration, hits the ground with his foot. However, Yazen looks back at William, "I wonder if that kid is the secret weapon that we need to win," says Yazen.

Chapter 4: The Fiend Hunter Headquarters

William awakens on a bed, looking around, he can see that the room is lit up by the sun outside, and he can see that the wallpaper is colored black, and a ceiling fan. William then looks at his ripped right arm, but his arm is back like it wasn't ripped off.

Then, from the door, he hears someone. "Are you awake, kid?" asks Yazen.

"Who are you? And where am I?" says William.

"Well, kid, my name is Yazen Alexander, the strongest fiend hunter of this era, and you're at the fiend hunter headquarters."

"Fiend Hunters, what are Fiend Hunters?" asks William.

"Fiend Hunters are warriors that hunt Fiends, and protect humans from the Fiends. Get up so I can show you around," says Yazen.

Yazen helps William stand up while walking through a hallway. He sees other people who look his age training, and he can see rooms filled with people who look like they're studying monsters and creatures.

One creature that William knows very well on the chalkboard is a Wendigo, and in another room, William can see a creature on a chalkboard, and the name of the creature is a skinwalker.

"Yazen, aren't those creatures from folklore?" asks William.

"Yes, they are," responds Yazen.

"Why are they learning about them?" asks William.

"Well, they have to learn about these creatures because we hunt those monsters, and they are the common ones that the new people hunt," answers Yazen.

William and Yazen walk into a larger room, and on the walls, William can see weapons. Yazen goes toward the wall with the weapons. "I believe a great weapon that suits you is these daggers," says Yazen.

The dagger William looks at is a dagger with a black handle, a blue blade, and orange lines on the blade. William looks at another set that has the same handle, but the blade is violet and has red lines. "Could I dual-weld daggers?" asks William.

"Yes, you may dual-weld daggers," responds Yazen.

When William looks at Yazen, he can see metal bracelets on both of his wrists, and William examines the weapon that Yazen has on his waist. The weapon looks like a Viking sword, and William examines what Yazen is wearing. Yazen is wearing a black sweater with purple lines that run down the side of the sweater and the arms. The pants color looks similar to the sweater's color, and Yazen also has a long turtle neck that reaches his chin, and looks like it's curved outward.

"Will I get a sweater or that type of clothing style like yours?" asks William.

"The clothing style you can pick, like the color, what you want on it, and other things you would like on it," says Yazen.

"Hey, sensi," someone says from behind William and Yazen. William and Yazen look behind.

"Hey Evan," says Yazen. William looks at Evan, who has a black sweater with a white turtle neck, and lines go from the turtle neck to the sleeves of the sweater, and the pants are white.

"Is this the new guy you told me about?" asks Evan.

"Yeah, his name is William Asher, William, this is Evan, Evan Lev," says Yazen.

"Hi!" says William excitedly.

Evan looks at William with a serious face. Yazen and Evan walk with William showing him the Headquarters, they show William a large field that looks similar to a school stadium field, next they show him a large room for training, the room has white walls and a grey floor, and the training room also has all kinds of practice weapons, finally they stop at a larger building.

"This building is the main headquarters for the Fiend Hunters," says Yazen.

"So, this building would be the main place for meetings," asks William.

Yazen nods. "Ok, sensei, I'll be on my way," says Evan.

Yazen and William wave at Evan walking away. Yazen and William walk into the building. William is amazed when he enters the building. There are three floors, there are people walking around with different uniforms, and walking with others. William also looks at the see-through room with people inside talking. Yazen and William walk towards a room. When William enters, he looks at a person sitting.

"The man sitting in front of you is the president of the Organization, we call him Prez," says Yazen.

"So, he's the founder of the organization," says William.

"No, he is the head of the organization, not the founder," says Yazen.

Then, the Prez gets up from the chair and walks up to William and Yazen. Prez greets William with a handshake.

"Hello, kid, you must be the new guy that William was telling me about," says Prez.

"Yes, sir," says William.

"So, William, do you understand why you are here at the Fiend Hunter Headquarters?" says Prez.

"No," William looks confused. Prez looks at Yazen with disappointment, but Yazen looks away.

"I hate when he looks at me with that face," Yazen tells himself.

"Well, William, you are here at the Fiend Hunter Headquarters because we sensed something about you. And we found out that you are a descendant of the king of the Fiends, and could be that chosen," says Prez.

William remembers back when Beelzebub told him that he was the chosen one.

"Hey, Kid, you alright? You look disturbed?" asks Prez.

"Well, back at the asylum, there was a demonic monster that said the same thing to me," says William.

"Do you remember what the name of this fiend is?" asks Prez.

"Yeah, I remember, his name is Beelzebub," says William.

"You fought against the third head of Lucifer's comrade," says Prez.

All William thought about was that he wanted to kill Beelzebub, and rip him piece by piece; he wanted to avenge his best friend Ben.

"All I want to do now is to get stronger so that I can kill Beelzebub and Lucifer from hurting and killing the weak. And so that no one else has to go through the same thing like me," says William.

"I will make you stronger, kid," Yazen tells himself.

"Well, kid, this is where your new life begins," says Prez.

"I will get stronger, will not give up, I will destroy you, Beelzebub," William tells himself.

Chapter 5: What Are Fiends?

"All right! Let's begin your training," says Yazen excitedly.

"All Right, Sensei! Help me become the strongest Sensei!" William says excitedly.

William and Yazen walk out of the Fiend Hunter Headquarters to the Training room.

"Ok, William, show me what you got," says Yazen.

"All right, Sensei," says William.

William then charges at Yazen, and thus begins William's training. A few moments later, William is on the floor, all bruised and tired.

"So, I see that you know some martial arts and boxing, but you need to get better with your speed and strength, kid," says Yazen.

The next few days after William's first day, William begins learning what monsters and demonic beings he'll face as a Fiend Hunter.

"Kid, as a Fiend hunter, you will face countless monsters and demonic beings, so I will teach you what you will be facing and how to defeat them, too," says Yazen.

"Well, I did fight some demonic monster in the asy…" Yazen interrupts William.

"Yes, those are some monsters that you will see again, but one thing I don't understand is how you defeated those two monsters?"

"What I remember is getting a boost of strength, which I call The Beast Within technique; however, when

Beelzebub appeared, he was stronger and faster than I was," says William.

"Yes, Beelzebub is way stronger than you are, but I can get stronger so that you can have a better chance at winning. Also, I will teach you how to fight with those daggers," says Yazen.

"YES, I can't wait to learn how to use these daggers," says William excitedly.

"Also, Will, do you like the clothing that I gave you?" asks Yazen.

"Yeah! I like the black color and purple lines on the sweater, and I like the black color of the pants too," says William.

"Anyways, let's get back to the lesson of these creatures. One of the creatures that you will encounter is a wendigo. These creatures are cannibals. A wendigo was once a human turned into a wendigo, and we have a theory of how people become wendigos. The theory goes that the Fiends that represent Gluttony and Greed cause the behavior of a human to cannibalize on other humans," says Yazen.

William then raises his hands. "Sensei, I have a question," says William.

"Yes, what is your question?" asks Yazen.

"Is there a way to help the person before they turn into a wendigo?" asks William.

"Yes, there is a way, but it will be difficult to help them. Let's get back to the lesson," Yazen says.

William then pays attention to Yazen with a serious face.

"Ok, other creatures that you will face are skinwalkers and fly heads. Unlike the wendigo, these creatures are not humans. These are entities that are created by the Fiends. The Skinwalker was created by the Fiends that represent Greed and Envy, the fly heads were created by the Fiend that represents Gluttony, Beelzebub is the Fiend who created the fly heads." Yazen says.

"So, if we defeat these fiends, will these creatures cease to exist?" asks William.

"No, even if we try, there will always be creatures that will exist," responds Yazen.

William, in frustration, clenches his fists. "Why do these Fiends exist? Why?" William tells himself in anger,

"Sensei, help me get stronger, so I can help others," William says.

Yazen smiles. "I will, kid," says Yazen.

Chapter 6: Training to become a Fiend Hunter

Another few weeks have passed by, and William and Yazen are walking towards the training facility.

"Ok, Will, you will be training on that rage technique today. You will need to control that technique so that you can use it against the Fiends and the creatures you will face as a hunter," says Yazen.

"Alright, Sensei!" William says excitedly.

Yazen and William sit on the floor and start meditating.

"Meditating will help you control that rage, so if you meditate every day, you will achieve that goal you're looking for," Yazen says.

William nods and starts meditating. Just then, William starts having visions of Ben dying at the hands of Beelzebub.

Beelzebub then looks at William, "You're a pathetic human. You couldn't save your friend. And you expect yourself to save others," Beelzebub says while chuckling.

William starts to get angry, he bites his lip in anger, which leads him to bleed from his lip, "I'LL KILL YOU BEELEZBUB!" William says in anger.

Then William awakens from his meditation by Yazen, and William starts looking around as if he's confused and disoriented.

"William, are you good?" Yazen says.

William looks at Yazen, "Yeah…I think I'm ok," William responds.

Yazen, in relief, says, "Ok, we'll stop for today, we'll train tomorrow, and you'll be sparring against someone tomorrow, alright."

William nods.

When William gets back to his dorm room, he gets ready to sleep. When William sleeps, he gets nightmares of Beelzebub killing Ben over and over again.

William awakens from his sleep, crying, "Why…Why…Why didn't I try to at least save Ben?" William says in anger and pain.

The next day, William gets up from his bed to change. After William exits his room, he starts walking to the training facility. When William enters the building

Yazen greets him, "Hey William, how are you doing? Are you feeling better than yesterday?" Yazen asks.

"I guess," says William.

Yazen nods, "Ok, first, William, I would like to introduce Mia. Mia Beatrix" Yazen says.

William looks at Mia, she has red hair, her sweater is grey with a black hoodie, and her pants are pure black.

"She is also new to this organization, like you are, but she's been here longer than you have," Yazen says, looking happy. "William, you'll be practicing with wooden daggers, and Mia will practice with a wooden sword," says William.

"I don't think it'll be fair if I use a dagger, right?" William says.

"Well, you are using daggers as your main weapon, sooo" says William while smiling. William rolls his eyes, "Ok, we'll get started now. If one of you gets taken down, then the round will end. Are both of you ready?" says William.

Both Mia and William nod. Mia grips her wooden sword hard, and William has one dagger reversed and the other forward. Then Mia and William get ready.

"Start," Yazen shouts.

Mia and William run towards each other. William uses a slicing movement at Mia, but Mia dodges the slices, then blocks a dagger with her sword, then Mia kicks William away, then Mia swings at William, and he dodges the swing. But then Mia sweeps William, causing him to fall, and Mia pokes William with the sword hard. "Ouch! Did you have to do that?" asks William.

Mia looks away from him, William sighs, Yazen claps his hands, "You got ruffled up, Will," says Yazen, smiling.

"You were distracted. That's why you lost," says Yazen.

Mia sighs, and William gets up to have another round against Mia. A few more rounds pass, William is on the ground, Mia sighed heavily, she then walks toward the door to leave, William then gets up fast, "Wait…I want to practice more. I want to get better. Please," William says.

Mia turns around, "Alright, but if you cry, it's not my problem, ok?" says Mia.

William smiles. In another place, Beelzebub is walking in a purple-red area. Beelzebub then stops, he kneels before the king of Fiend Lucifer, "My king, I have returned. And I have joyful news, my king," says Beelzebub while chuckling,

Lucifer gets annoyed by Beelzebub's laughter. "SHUT IT!" says Lucifer.

Beelzebub stops laughing, but leaves a grin.

"Now. You may speak," says Lucifer.

"My king. I have found the chosen," says Beelzebub, still grinning.

Lucifer smiles ear to ear. "That's nice to hear."

Chapter 7: The Fiend Hunter Meeting

Four weeks later, William wakes up and quickly changes to train with Yazen. Just then, he hears a knock at the door.

"I'll be there in a bit!" says William, rushing.

William opens the door to find Yazen waiting.

"Good morning, William," says Yazen.

"Morning," William responds.

"Today, we're not training. We have something more important than training," says Yazen.

William is a bit shocked. "Oh… okay then."

"Alright, let's get moving," says Yazen.

While walking, William looks at Yazen and notices he always wears a bucket hat.

"Hey Sensei, I have a question," asks William.

"Yeah? What's your question?" Yazen replies.

"Why do you always wear a bucket hat all the time, even though you have all that white hair?" William asks.

Yazen pauses. "Well, I like wearing this hat. But not only that—this hat was from my best friend. He became what he hated. He betrayed the organization… and most of all, he betrayed me."

He speaks in a serious but sad tone. William, hearing what Yazen said, feels guilty for asking.

"Anyway," Yazen continues, "like I said before—we're not training. We're going to a meeting. The Fiend Hunter meeting."

"What's the meeting for?" William asks.

"Well, it depends. It can either be something to do with you, or it might involve important missions that they're going to explain to us," says Yazen.

"Okay," responds William.

They arrive at the Fiend Hunter headquarters. Upon entering the building, an assistant is waiting for them.

"Both of you, follow me. I'll lead you to the meeting," says the assistant.

William and Yazen follow the assistant up to the third floor. The assistant opens the door for them. William enters first and sees a lot of people in the room.

He notices someone wielding a Viking-like axe, another person with a gun on his hip and a sword, and also sees Evan and Mia. In the middle of the room stands Prez.

"Okay, hopefully this is everyone," says Prez. "I called every Fiend Hunter here because we have leads on Lucifer and his subordinates. And we have discovered something horrible."

Everyone listens attentively.

"We have intel that there are *new* creatures we have to worry about. These creatures, we believe, were created by Lucifer. They are other types of fiends, ones that never existed until now. So we think they are entities created by him."

He continues, "Because of these new creatures, more people are dying than ever before. So what we are planning is to send teams of hunters to different places to handle these fiends and whatever else you find there. Does anyone have any questions?"

No one responds.

"Alright then. Everyone will get a location and a team assignment when the meeting is done."

When the meeting ends, everyone starts preparing for their missions. Yazen walks up to William.

"William, follow me," says Yazen.

William nods and follows. When they exit the building, Yazen speaks.

"I'll be putting you in a team, okay? So don't worry about it."

"Okay. Who are you going to put me with?" asks William.

"Well, I think Mia and Evan will be a good fit for your team—and you know them too," says Yazen.

"Okay. And what location will I be going to with Mia and Evan?" William asks.

"Your team will be going to Schiller Woods in Chicago. There have been reports of missing people, so we suspect it might be wendigos, skinwalkers, demons, or some other monster," says Yazen in a serious tone.

William looks at Yazen in confusion. "Wait, what do you mean by 'other monsters'? I thought it was just fiends, wendigos, skinwalkers, and fly heads?"

"Well," says Yazen, "there could be other monsters—creatures made by Lucifer or other strong fiends. So, you never really know what they're doing in that other world of fiends. Please, William… be careful, alright?"

William nods.

When they reach William's dorm, William asks one last question.

"Yazen, I have a question."

Yazen looks back. "Yeah, hit me."

William then asks, "If you were to fight Lucifer one-on-one, would you prevail?"

Yazen smiles. "Well, Lucifer would give me a good fight. But if I removed my metal bracelets, I'd be stronger than I am now."

"Then… would you still fail to defeat him?" asks William.

Yazen replies confidently, "No. I'll win."

Epilogue

"I need to get out of this damn place," the man said, running through the darkness of the forest. His heart felt like it was about to burst out of his chest. Sweat poured down his face, blurring his vision as he glanced around in panic.

Suddenly, he heard a stick crack behind him. Fear tightening in his chest, he turned slowly—only to find nothing there. Letting out a shaky breath, he muttered, "I think… I lost that monster." Relief washed over him for a moment.

Then came the pain—sharp, stabbing, and unbearable—in his belly. Looking down, his eyes widened in horror. A large, gaping wound split his abdomen open. His intestines glistened in the moonlight. Agony overtook him, and he collapsed to the forest floor.

The sound of sticks snapping came from every direction. His breath quickened as he searched for the source. To his left, a figure emerged—pure white and humanoid in shape, but grotesquely unnatural. Its arms and legs were so thin the bones were visible beneath the skin. Its hands were huge, tipped with long, sharp nails, and its feet were elongated beyond human proportions. Its torso was skeletal, as if it hadn't eaten in months.

But its face was the most terrifying of all. Long, tangled hair hung from its head. Its ears were pointed at the tips. Its eyes were a dull, lifeless grey. Its elongated nose and mouth were filled with a disturbing mix of sharp animal-like teeth and crooked human ones.

From his right, another pure-white creature stepped into view, nearly identical to the first. It smiled—wide and unnatural—baring those horrifying teeth. Then it spoke, mimicking the voice of the man's companion.

"He… lp… us," it croaked.

"SHUT UP!" the man screamed, shaking his head violently. He kept repeating the words—"Shut up, shut up, shut up"—until his voice became a whisper, madness setting in.

The creatures charged. His screams echoed through the forest as they descended on him, clawing and tearing into his flesh. Blood sprayed across the trees and plants, pooling beneath his writhing body. He coughed up blood, gasping in agony, until at last his cries went silent.

Still, the creatures kept ripping and devouring his remains.

Then—headlights. A vehicle pulled up nearby. The creatures froze, listening. In one final motion, they tore the man's body in half, then slipped away into the shadows to stalk their next prey.

The adventure begins now...

www.ingramcontent.com/pod-product-compliance
Lightning Source LLC
Chambersburg PA
CBHW071215300726

48975CB00004B/1317